Keiko Kasza

The Pigs' Picnic

G.P. Putnam's Sons   New York

Copyright © 1988 by Keiko Kasza
All rights reserved. This book, or parts thereof,
may not be reproduced in any form without
permission in writing from the publishers.
Published simultaneously in Canada.
Printed in Hong Kong by South China Printing Co.
Designed by Martha Rago.
First impression

Library of Congress Cataloging-in-Publication Data
Kasza, Keiko.
The pigs' picnic / Keiko Kasza.
p. cm.
Summary: Mr. Pig, on his way to call on Miss Pig,
allows his animal friends to persuade him to don
various handsome portions of their own bodies,
with an alarming result.
ISBN 0-399-21543-3
[1. Pigs—Fiction. 2. Animals—Fiction.
3. Identity—Fiction.] I. Title.
PZ7.K15645Pi 1988   87-22691
[E]—dc19   CIP
                                  AC

To Edward Kosuke Kasza

It was a perfect day for a picnic. Mr. Pig tried to look his best. He was going to ask Miss Pig to go on a picnic with him.

"Gee, I hope she says 'yes,'" thought Mr. Pig. But he was worried, so he took a flower to impress her.

On the way to Miss Pig's house, he met his friend the Fox. When the Fox heard about the picnic, he said, "Let me give you some advice, Mr. Pig. Borrow my beautiful tail."

"There, you see how foxy you look?
Miss Pig will like that," said the Fox.
Mr. Pig was pleased.

Then he met his friend the Lion. When
the Lion heard about the picnic, he said,
"Let me give you some advice, Mr. Pig.
Borrow my beautiful hair."

"There, you see how courageous you look? Miss Pig will like that," said the Lion. Mr. Pig was pleased.

Then he met his friend the Zebra. When
the Zebra heard about the picnic, he said,
"Let me give you some advice, Mr. Pig.
Borrow my beautiful stripes."

"There, you see how handsome you look? Miss Pig will like that," said the Zebra. Mr. Pig was pleased. He had never felt so handsome.

He finally arrived at Miss Pig's house and knocked on the door.

"Will you go on a picnic with me?" he asked.

Miss Pig was shocked. "Oh, no!" she said. "Who is this monster? If you don't go away, I'll call Mr. Pig. He will take care of you."

Mr. Pig ran back the way he came.
He returned the tail to the Fox, the hair
to the Lion, and the stripes to the Zebra.

And then he hurried back to Miss Pig's house, and once more he knocked on the door.

"Will you go on a picnic with me?" he asked again.

"Oh, Mr. Pig!" she cried. "I'm so glad to see you. Just now there was an ugly monster right here in this yard. I'd love to go on a picnic with you, Mr. Pig."

All the way to the picnic, Miss Pig talked about the monster who had visited her house. Her handsome friend Mr. Pig listened sympathetically.

It was a perfect day for a picnic.